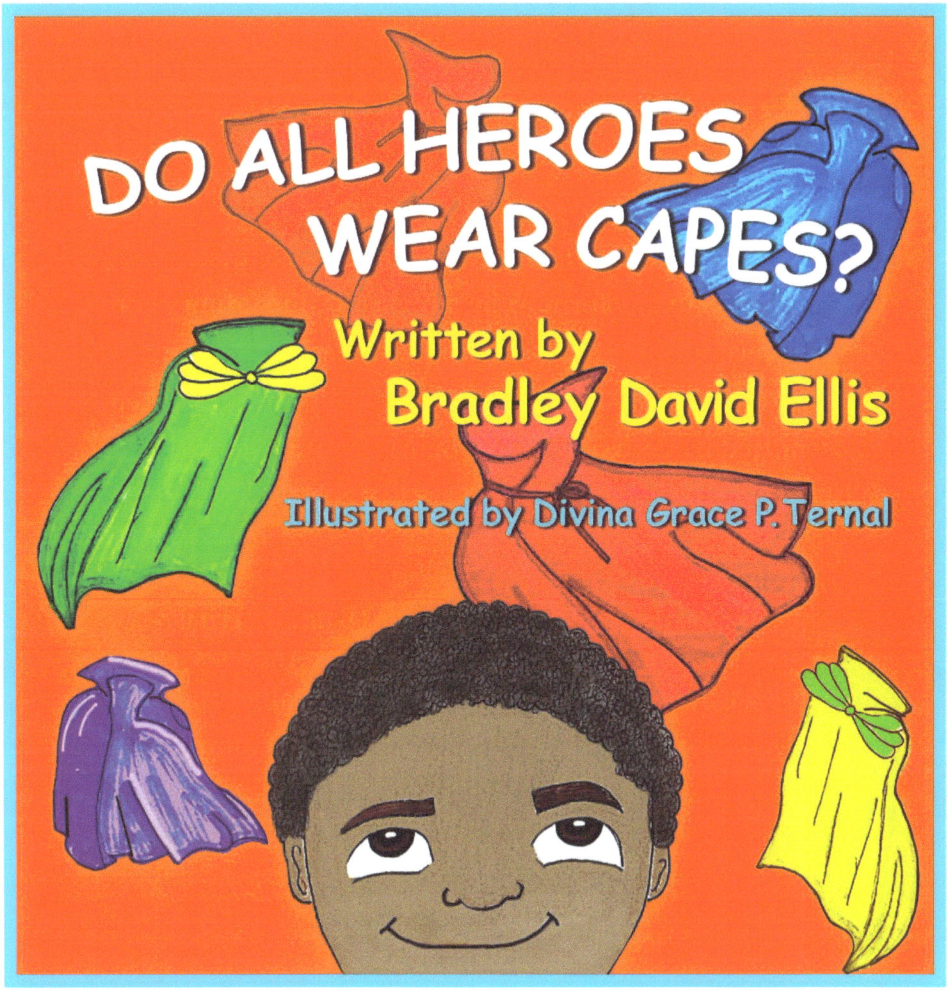

DO ALL HEROES WEAR CAPES?

Written by
Bradley David Ellis

Illustrated by Divina Grace P. Ternal

Illustrations by Divina Grace P. (Bambi) Ternal
Publishing Guidance with Heather Andrews
Book Cover and Layout Design by Lorie Miller Hansen
Digital ePub design and creation by Andrea Cinnamond

ISBN (paperback) 978-1-0688037-2-7
ISBN (electronic) 978-1-0688037-0-3

First Edition, printed July 2024

DEDICATION

*I dedicate this book to all the people who
are heroic everyday despite not wearing a utility
belt, tights, or a cape and to Mrs. Mary Baldwin
who every day, every year, was a hero to everyone
at AHS and in-turn, made everyone
at AHS feel like a hero.*

Thank you Mrs. B, rest in peace. 

Stephen was a comic book fan. Actually, he was more than a fan—he was a **fanatic.**

No matter the comic book, he had read it.
    He knew all the characters' names, their powers, and their weaknesses. **He even knew the villains.**

Stephen always wanted to be a superhero.

He wanted to fly through the air and jump over buildings. He pictured himself throwing buses and running so fast he became invisible— **all while stopping the bad guys.**

His dream of being a superhero had two problems. First, there was no such thing as a superhero, and second, he was only ten years old.

Still, these complications didn't stop Stephen from trying to be a **superhero.**

One day, he told his best friend, Malik,
"You know, if **I'm going to be a superhero**,
I should probably start training now."

Malik frowned. "Stephen, people can't
really fly or become invisible.
You know that, right?"

"Well, sure, people can't do those
things without a little practice
but I know I can be a superhero,
so I need to start training now.
Do you want to help?"
Stephen asked.

Malik sighed.
He knew he couldn't
change his friend's mind.

"Well, I am your best friend, so of course I'll help, but we'll have to start another day. It's almost supper time, so I have to go home."

The boys separated to walk home. On the way, Stephen saw Thao...

Thao was thin and short for her age, which made her an easy target for the school bullies.

Stephen saw that the bullies had taken her backpack and hung her violin in a tree, up too high for her to reach. They taunted her, teased her, and pushed her to the ground. When she finally broke into tears, they ran off, laughing.

Stephen ran over to her and helped her up. "Don't pay attention to them, Thao. I like you. You have a really nice laugh, and you are so good at the violin."

"Thank you, Stephen, you are so kind," Thao replied.

With that, Stephen climbed the tree and slowly crawled out onto the branch to retrieve her violin.

"Please be careful, Stephen. I don't want you to fall and get hurt," Thao said nervously.

"I'll be fine," Stephen replied, focusing on the violin.

A few moments later, he jumped down and handed the violin to Thao.

"Thank you so much, Stephen," she said.

"No problem," Stephen replied, and he continued his journey home...

Every Saturday, Stephen played soccer with his friends in the park. He was an average player, so he was never the first pick, but he didn't mind. He was just happy to play. After each game, Stephen walked home and passed Mr. Errington's small corner store.

Mr. Errington knew exactly what Stephen bought after every soccer match—a bottle of water and an apple. Today was no different, so Stephen munched on his apple and sipped his water as he continued home.

When Stephen turned the corner, he saw Miss Darby walking down the street. She was carrying two bags of groceries, but the bags were not going to last much longer.

"Hi, Miss Darby. Nice day today, isn't it?" Stephen called out.

Just as Miss Darby turned around, both bags broke, and her groceries fell to the ground.

"Oh, would you look at that?" Miss Darby said.

"I can help you with those, Miss Darby," Stephen said as he scooped up her groceries and put them in his gym bag.

"Well, aren't you a dear?" Miss Darby said with a smile.

"It is so nice of you to help me with these. I'm only two blocks away from home, but I doubt I would've made it there by myself—not with my groceries, anyway."

"It's no problem, Miss Darby," Stephen replied. "You see, I'm going to be a superhero someday, so I need to train now to build my muscles. This is practice."

Miss Darby just laughed and said, "Thank you, all the same."

At Miss Darby's house,
Stephen unloaded his
bag and started for
the door,
 "See you,
 Miss Darby."

"Oh wait, Stephen," Miss Darby said. "I want to give you something to say thank you for your help today."

"You don't have to do that, Miss Darby. It was my pleasure." Miss Darby smiled, and Stephen darted out the door.

The rest of Stephen's weekend was routine; homework, household chores, and dinner with his family, but he couldn't stop thinking about Monday. Would the school bullies pick on Thao again, or would they bully a new person? Maybe they would go after him. He smiled at that thought. That would be good superhero training.

On Monday morning, Stephen discovered that the bullies had found a new target—"Nerdy" Nick.

Nick was originally from England, so he sounded different from everyone else. Nick knew a lot about the British Navy, but that didn't help him with his classmates. Nick could name all the ships from the royal navy, and he liked to call himself Saxon.

Stephen watched as the bullies shoved Nick. He tried to fight back, but six against one were not good numbers—**unless you were a superhero**.

Stephen sprinted toward the mob, hollering, "Leave him alone, you bullies!" He pushed one boy aside and helped Nick stand. Stephen then turned to the leader of the group, Matt. The boys eyed each other. Stephen pushed Matt and yelled, "Quit picking on people!"

Suddenly, the whole gang of boys turned toward Stephen.

"Run, Nick! Get the teachers. **I'll hold them off**!"

Stephen was determined to make his stand, but the boys overwhelmed him. Stephen was lying on the ground, and just as the group closed in on him, Mr. Parks yelled out, "All of you! Stop fighting, and come with me right now!"

Stephen peered around the boys and saw Nick standing beside Mr. Parks.

"Stephen started it," Matt said.

Mr. Parks frowned. "Six against one, and he started it? Try again, Mr. Shaw."

Stephen didn't reply.

At the principal's office, all the boys got a lecture about playing nice, and afterward, she assigned them detention for two days. Even though Stephen got detention, he didn't complain. At least he stopped the bullies from hurting Nick.

On the way home that day, Stephen saw Nathan sitting on the side of the road beside his bike, which had two flat tires.

"Hey, Nate. Let me help you there," Stephen called out.

"Oh, hi, Stephen," Nate called back. "That would be great. It's a lot easier to ride bikes than to push them—especially with two flat tires!"

Stephen was confident that his superhero strength could help Nate push the bike home. The bike was heavy, but Stephen couldn't let Nate down. Superheroes don't quit because they're tired.

Six blocks and two rest stops later, they arrived at Nate's house. "Thanks, Buddy. I really appreciate it," Nate said.

"Not a problem. It's what I do," Stephen said proudly in between breaths.

"Do you want some water?" Nate offered politely.

"Nope. I have to get home. Mom's expecting me soon, so I have to hustle," Stephen replied, and he darted home.

The rest of the week was disappointing because nothing bad happened, so Stephen didn't get a chance to practice being a superhero. At least he had his class trip to look forward to. That weekend, they were going to Super-Happy-Fun Land, the best amusement park around.

The day of the trip, the weather was great, and the park wasn't too crowded. Malik and Stephen were excited to try the super-cool new rides. They joined a group on the whirly tilt, which spun in two directions, rotated in a circle, and moved up and down. It was a blast. The kids screamed with glee.

As they were climbing out of their seats, Nicole jumped down and hit the curb, twisting her ankle. "Owwwww! My ankle," Nicole yelled.

The group looked around for a teacher or parent, but they were all supervising the first and second graders.

"It's okay. I'm going to get you help," Stephen said.

He knew what he had to do. "Help me, Malik." Stephen and Malik scooped Nicole up from the sidewalk, and Stephen piggybacked her all the way to the first-aid station.

The nurse wrapped up Nicole's ankle tightly and told her she'd be okay. Stephen was relieved.

"Are you sure you're okay, Nicole?" Stephen asked.

"Yes. It doesn't hurt anymore. Thank you for what you did," Nicole replied.

"Can you walk?" Stephen asked.

"Yep! I'm ready to get to the roller coasters," Nicole said, smiling.

"Then let's go!" Thao said from the corner.

The next Wednesday, after school, Stephen and his friends were walking home when they saw a beautiful orange and white cat. Stephen had seen the cat before—this cat often greeted students on their way home.

Just as he was about to pet the cat, Stephen saw a woman walking her dog—a big dog.

The dog took one look at that cat, let out a howl, and broke its leash.

"Meeeooooowwwww!"

The cat screeched and sprinted toward the nearest tree, with the dog right behind her. The kitty scrambled up high in the tree, and the dog looked up, barking loudly. Finally, the dog's owner tied the leash back together and pulled the dog down the street.

A few minutes later, an elderly man walked down the street, yelling, "Blossom!"

"Excuse me, sir," Stephen said. "Are you looking for your cat?"

"I sure am. Have you seen her?"

Stephen pointed up at the tree. "I think she's stuck," he replied.

"Okay. I'll get my ladder from the garage," the man said.

"I can get her down for you," Stephen told him.

"No, son. I can get her. She's done this before.

You just stay there and watch Blossom until I get back, please," the nice man called over his shoulder.

Stephen looked up and said, "I can get her down."

"Yo, Stephen," Malik immediately said. "Bad idea. That's a real bad idea. Just wait for him to come back with the ladder. It's his cat."

"Yeah, Stephen," Nicole echoed. "She's really high up. That's dangerous."

"I can do it," Stephen said confidently, and without another thought, he was climbing up the tree.

As he approached the branch where Blossom was holding on for dear life, Stephen cooed, "Come here, kitty. I'm here to save you."

Blossom backed up further away from Stephen toward the end of the branch.

"Please come back, Stephen," Malik pleaded.

"If you fall, we can't catch you!"

"I'm fine. Come back, kitty," Stephen replied in one breath.

"Meoowww."

Stephen crawled out a little bit more, close enough to touch Blossom. Just then, Blossom panicked and scratched Stephen's hand. Stephen yelled, lost his grip, and plummeted out of the tree, landing flat on his back.

"I think I broke my whole body," Stephen moaned.

"Are you okay?" Nicole asked gingerly.

"No... I think I really hurt myself," Stephen said with curiosity.

He couldn't believe it. How could this have happened?

He was a superhero. He'd been practicing hard!

Superheroes are not supposed to get hurt. They are not supposed to fall out of trees.

They—Are—Not—Supposed—To—Fail.

Malik looked down at Stephen. "Do you need to go to the hospital?"

"I don't know, but it hurts—my back, my neck, my arms, my knees. They all hurt."

As if things couldn't get worse, Matt, the bully, was watching from across the parking lot. "Forget something, loser?" Matt yelled tauntingly. "So where's the cat? Dork!"

"Leave him alone," Malik said. "At least he tried."

"Do you really think you're some kind of hero? You're nothing but a wannabe who runs around pretending," Matt shouted.

Stephen hit his breaking point. Between the pain of falling and hearing Matt taunt him, he couldn't hold it back. Tears streamed down his face.

"Oh, look! The little baby is crying. Boo hoo hoo." With that, Matt walked away, laughing.

A few minutes later, the nice man came back with his ladder just as Mr. Parks came out to see why everyone was gathered around the tree.

"Oh, Stephen, what did you do? Let's get you inside and cleaned-up," Mr. Parks said.

"Stephen tried to get the cat out of the tree, Mr. Parks," Nicole said.

"I told them to leave Blossom in the tree and that I was getting a ladder," the elderly man said, pushing the ladder against the tree.

"I am sure you did, Sir. Is your cat alright?" Mr. Parks asked.

"She looks fine from here. You just take care of your student," the man said. In a jiffy, he climbed up the ladder and brought Blossom down with him.

As Mr. Parks carried Stephen inside the school to call his parents, Stephen tried to hide his tears from his friends because superheroes don't cry.

Inside, the nurse cleaned the scratches on Stephen's hands, knees, and elbows. She gave him an ice pack for the bump on his head. Then, she bandaged the cuts and sent him to the principal's office.

Inside the principal's office, Mrs. Khalil was talking
to his parents on the phone.

"Yes, Sir, he is here now. I think he's fine. The nurse said it was just a few bumps, scrapes, and bruises. Of course, I think you should keep an eye on him, but I think his pride hurts most of all.

Thank you. Yes, Sir. Goodbye, Mr. Townsend."
Mrs. Khalil hung-up the phone and looked at Stephen.
"Your dad's on his way, but it looks like we
need to have a talk."

"Yes, Mrs. Khalil," Stephen said sheepishly.

"Do you understand why that man asked you to leave his cat
in the tree and to let the adults handle it?"
Mrs. Khalil asked softly.

"I thought I could do it. I just wanted to help,"
Stephen said.

"I understand why you tried, but that doesn't answer
the question. Do you see how bad this was and how
it could have been worse?"

Stephen didn't answer.

"You could have scared the cat, and it could have been hurt.
You were hurt, and you could have been hurt so much
worse. You were lucky, young man," Mrs. Khalil
said a little more strongly.

"But **superheroes always help**, and **they always save the day**," Stephen said sheepishly.

"Yes, they do, but superheroes only exist in comic books. Stephen, you are a nice boy, a good student, and helpful to everyone. We all see that, but let the adults take care of the dangerous situations, and you just keep being the good little boy you are."

"Yes, I understand," Stephen said quietly.

"Very good. Now, please go wait in the office lobby for your dad. You are excused from coming to school tomorrow if your parents feel you need to stay home," Mrs. Khalil said, clearly ending the conversation.

Stephen stood and shuffled into the lobby, where Nate, Nick, Nicole, Thao, and Malik were waiting on him.

"Hey, buddy. Are you okay?" Malik asked.

"We were really worried about you," Thao said, not waiting for Stephen to answer.

"You are important to us," Nick said quickly. "You stick up for us. Don't think we don't notice."

Nate jumped in. "Yeah, you're kind and helpful."

"Well... I..." Stephen said.

"Just stay who you are and be there for us. You don't have to save us. You just have to be the good guy we know you are," Nicole said sweetly.

"Thanks, everyone," Stephen said, feeling better. "But I am sorry you saw me cry."

"Why?" Malik immediately asked. "Anyone would be crying if they fell out of a tree and hit the ground as hard as you did."

"So you don't think I'm a baby?" Stephen asked.

"Nah," Malik said. "You have nothing to worry about from us."

With that, his friends said goodbye and headed home.

Luckily, Stephen didn't have to wait long in the quiet lobby because his dad arrived a few minutes later.

"Well, son, it looks like you had a day. Ready to go home?"
his dad asked.

"Sure, Dad," Stephen said, slowly rising from his chair.
"Stephen, on the way home, I think we should go by Creamy
Cold Ice Cream. What do you think?" his dad asked with
a smile, winking at
Stephen.

"Yeah, Dad.
I think that
sounds great."
Stephen smiled.

 "Okay, let's go, Buddy,"
    his Dad said and exited the lobby.

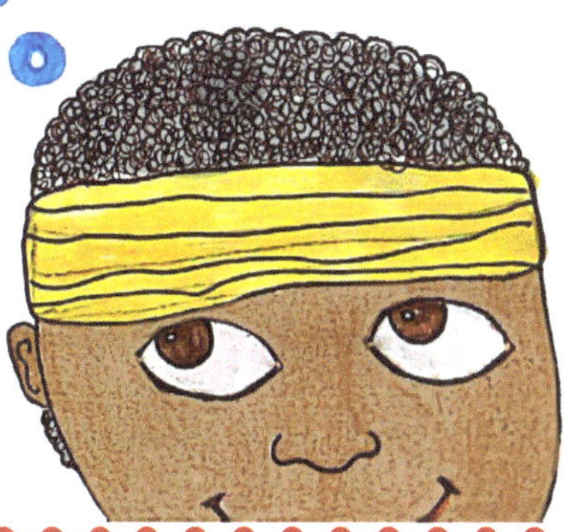

Just then, the secretary looked up from behind her desk.

"You know, Stephen, you have great friends, and that's because you're a wonderful young man. I know how you are always willing to help. I saw how you helped Miss Darby with her groceries and how you are always there for anyone, regardless of what it costs you," Mrs. Baldwin said kindly.

"Really, you know about that?" Stephen asked.

"Of course I do. I'm the school secretary. I know everything that goes on around here," she said with a twinkle in her eye.

"Thanks," Stephen said, and he grabbed the door handle.

"Oh, and Stephen?" Mrs. Baldwin added.

"Yes?"

"You don't need to wear a cape or have superpowers to be a hero." She then went back to her typing.

"Thank you, Mrs. Baldwin," Stephen said, feeling ten feet tall.

Wow,
Stephen thought
to himself.

I'm already a hero.
Being kind and
helping others
is heroic...

...I knew I'd be
a superhero one day!

The End

ACKNOWLEDGEMENTS

All glory goes to God, for through God all
things are possible, Amen. I thank God for giving me the
inspiration and perseverance when I needed them most.
I believe he worked through His own intervention and
through the following people;

Thanks to my family for their encouragement and support. Thanks to
my production team of Heather Andrews, Lorie Miller Hansen, Andrea
Cinnamond, Bambi, Lizzie and Rhose. Thanks to Jennifer Traynor for
introducing me to Heather and thanks to Jenn Kelly for introducing me to
Jennifer Traynor. Further thanks to Dr. Milan-Devi LaBrey for being the first
to encourage me to embark on this passion.

Thanks to my backers, both emotionally and financially, along this journey.

...and finally thanks to you, the reader for taking a chance on an
unknown author who felt he had stories to tell.

——I **HAVE LIVED** a life split between two hemispheres. Born in Scarbourough and raised in Ajax, Ontario, I graduated from Carleton University and Algonquin College—eventually landing in Incheon, South Korea, where I became an "English as a foreign language" teacher for 18 years.

These days I split my time between Forest, Ontario and Port Hope, Ontario. I have a wide-range of interests including sports, photography, history, re-enacting history, and cooking. One quirk, I am horribly afraid of heights.

———I am **DIVINA GRACE TERNAL (Bambi)**, a 35-year-old wife, and mother of three adorable children. I am currently living in the city of Manila and work in the administrative staff of an online sales group.

I would like to acknowledge the author of the book Bradley Ellis, and thank him for entrusting me to make the drawings of this book.

To my family, thank you for the unconditional love and support for being my avid fans and most of all to our almighty God, who gave me the talent, and perseverance to finish this beautiful book. Thanks also to Lizzie and Rhose for recommending me to Bradley.

To God be all the Glory! Amen.